It is February of 1949 in Clear River, Nebraska. Addie Mills, now thirteen, is certain no one else has ever had to cope with the problems she is going through. Certainly no one, especially her "immature" friends, could possibly understand her special feelings for Mr. Davenport, their new seventh-grade teacher. Addie borrows his personal art books and devoutly lingers after school just to be near him.

Her friends tease her about her crush, but to Addie it's not silly and childish at all, the way crushes are thought to be. Addie misunderstands her own feelings about Mr. Davenport and also about Billy Wild, a boy her own age, and she is soon caught up in a whirl of confusion about love. Life is further complicated by her discovery of her stern father's new girlfriend, and her grandmother's revealed secret of her own first love.

In this fourth book about Addie Mills, Gail Rock once again writes with a special warmth and understanding which today's young readers are certain to welcome.

Other books by Gail Rock

The Thanksgiving Treasure
The House Without a Christmas Tree
A Dream for Addie

Addie and the King of Hearts

by Gail Rock

Alfred A. Knopf ✦ New York

THIS IS A BORZOI BOOK PUBLISHED BY ALFRED A. KNOPF, INC.

Library of Congress Cataloging in Publication Data

Rock, Gail Addie and the King of Hearts

SUMMARY: Addie's feelings for her handsome seventh grade teacher are focused toward the Valentine's dance when she hopes to impress him with her sophistication. [1. St. Valentine's Day—Fiction] I. McVicker, Charles. II. Title PZ7.R587Ad3. [Fic] 75–35776 ISBN 0–394–83228–0 ISBN 0–394–93228–5 lib. bdg.

Manufactured in the United States of America 10 9 8 7 6 5 4 3 2 1

With thanks to Addie's good friends,
Alan Shayne and Pat Ross.

Addie and the King of Hearts

Prologue

I'M AN ARTIST NOW, and I live and work in the city. It's a landscape of cement and noise and crowds—all very different from the little town where I grew up.

In the city I hardly realize it's Valentine's Day until the shops display ready-made cards, and the bakeries turn out heart-shaped cakes and cookies to take home at the last minute. But when I was growing up in Nebraska in the 1940s, I looked forward to Valentine's Day for weeks. I cut hearts from paper doilies and composed funny verses for them, and I saved my allowance to buy red satin boxes full of chocolates. When the day finally arrived, it was always a contest with my friends to see who got the most valentines.

But the Valentine's Day I remember best was in 1949 when I was thirteen. That was when I first found out about love.

Chapter One

WE WERE MILLING AROUND the seventh-grade classroom that morning, laughing and talking. For once, almost all of us had been early. It was the first day back in school after the Christmas–New Year's holiday, and there was a lot of talk about what we all got for Christmas, and about the fantastic blizzards that had been smothering Nebraska that winter.

The main topic of conversation, however, was speculation about the new teacher we would meet that morning. Miss Collins, who had started teaching our class that fall, had decided to get married over the holidays. All the other girls thought that was very romantic, but I just thought it was stupid. Lots of the kids in our class were starting to exchange rings and "go steady," and I hated all that mush. The whole idea made me laugh. I planned to grow up and be an artist and never get married.

I was sitting on top of my desk talking to my best friend, Carla Mae Carter. Carla Mae and her big family lived next door to my dad and grandmother and me, and we had been friends for years. My worst friend, Tanya Smithers, came hurrying through the door. Tanya had been my worst friend ever since I could remember. We annoyed each other a lot, but we continued to be a part of the same group. There were only 1,500 people in the town of Clear River, so sometimes you didn't have a big choice of friends. Tanya planned to be a famous ballet dancer when she grew up, and she was always twirling around on her toes or striking some dramatic pose to remind us all of how talented she was.

"Here comes Pavlova," said Carla Mae when she saw Tanya coming toward us.

"If she tells me one more time that she got new ballet shoes for Christmas, I'll scream!" I said.

"Addie! Carla Mae!" Tanya said to us breathlessly. "Guess what I just heard when I went by the principal's office?"

"The principal got new ballet shoes for Christmas?" I asked sarcastically.

Carla Mae snickered.

"No, you idiots!" said Tanya. "Listen to me! We're getting a *man* teacher to replace Miss Collins!"

"What?" said Carla Mae. "You've gotta be kidding!"

"A man!" I said. "Yuck! That's awful!"

"We've never had a man teacher," said Carla Mae. "There aren't any in the whole school!"

"I don't believe it!" I said.

"I'm telling you it's true!" said Tanya, annoyed. "The principal says he's going to be here in a few minutes."

The rumor spread around the room as others overheard our conversation.

"Oh, ugh!" I said. "He'll probably be an old grouch."

"Tanya, what does he look like?" Carla Mae asked.

"I don't know," Tanya answered. "I didn't see him. But I heard his name. It's Davenport."

"Like the sofa?" asked Carla Mae.

"He's probably covered with horsehair," I said, laughing. "He's probably a million years old with a beard and warts!"

I got up and hobbled around as though I were an old man with a cane, and everybody laughed.

Suddenly Jimmy Walsh shot a paper airplane across the room at us and I grabbed it in midflight, making a spectacular catch. I was good at that sort of thing.

"That's Billy Wild's New Year's resolution!" Jimmy shouted to me.

"It is not!" shouted Billy from across the room. "He made it up! It's his!"

Everybody was always teasing me about liking Billy Wild, and I always insisted I didn't. I had to admit he was tall and handsome—with dark curly hair and blue eyes—and that he was one of the smartest boys in the class, and good at sports. But that didn't mean I liked him any more than anyone else. He was forever strutting around in his cowboy boots, showing off. We had known each other for years and we still always seemed to be arguing about something, so I didn't see how anyone could say I liked him.

I unfolded the paper airplane and read it to myself, then burst out laughing.

"OK, attention, everybody!" I shouted, running to the front of the classroom. "Here's Billy Wild's New Year's resolution!"

"It is not!" he shouted again.

Everyone was laughing, and I climbed up on top of the teacher's desk to read it aloud.

"Dated January 1, 1949," I read. "I, Billy Wild, resolve for 1949 to kiss every girl in the seventh-grade class."

Everyone screamed with laughter, and Billy's face got bright red.

"It's not mine!" he shouted.

"That's one resolution you'll never keep!" I shouted, and folded the airplane, then shot it back in his direction.

Suddenly everyone stopped laughing and the room fell quiet. I couldn't imagine what was happening; and then I realized that they were all looking at something behind me. I turned.

There standing just inside the door was a tall, blond, handsome, young man. For a moment I thought I must have seen him in the movies; then I realized that he looked a bit like Alan Ladd. Of course he had to be the new teacher. And he had found me standing on his desk, flying paper airplanes!

I stood there frozen. Miss Collins would have dragged me to the principal's office. He just smiled. He had a wonderful smile and crinkly blue eyes. I thought he was the most handsome man I had ever seen. I suddenly realized I was still standing on top of his desk.

"May I help you down?" he said to me.

He extended his hand and helped me down as the class snickered behind me. I was numb with embarrassment, both at being found on top of his desk and at the way he looked. He was so attractive that I felt I should look away.

"Won't you have a seat?" he said, and I sheepishly went back to my desk. I knew I should say something to him, but I was tongue-tied. That was not at all like me.

"My name is Douglas Davenport," he said to the class, "and I'm your new teacher." He turned to the board and wrote his name there.

Carla Mae, who sat behind me, leaned forward and whispered to me.

"Is he gorgeous? I don't believe it!"

I didn't say anything. I was still speechless.

Tanya leaned over to join in the conversation from her desk across the aisle.

"He is an absolute doll!" she said.

Mr. Davenport turned back to the class and noticed a water-color hanging on the wall near his desk.

"Did someone in the class do this painting?" he asked.

I opened my mouth, but no sound came out.

Carla Mae spoke up behind me.

"Addie Mills did it," she said, pointing to me. "She's the best artist in the class."

"Oh, the paper airplane pilot," Mr. Davenport said, smiling at me again.

Everyone laughed, and my face burned.

He was still smiling at me.

"Well, Addie," he said. "I can tell you're very talented. Studying art is one of my hobbies. I'll have to talk to you more about that."

Carla Mae swooned behind me and whispered, "You lucky dog!"

I just sat there staring at Mr. Davenport and feeling strange.

In the next few weeks we all got to know Mr. Davenport better, and it was soon clear that he was to be one of the most popular teachers our class had ever had.

All the girls agreed that he was an absolute dish, and though the boys thought we were ridiculous for gushing about him, they liked him a lot, too. We discovered that he was only twenty-four years old, that he drove a tan Chevrolet convertible coupe with white sidewall tires, and that he wore neat, tweedy suits and incredible argyle socks, and smoked a pipe. We spent hours discussing these little details about him, and I collected this information more avidly than anyone, though I never let on.

The strange feeling that had stricken me when I first saw Mr. Davenport still lingered whenever I would talk with him.

I talked with him often. I felt I had much more in common with him than the other kids in the class. Somehow I was more grown-up than they were, and I was able to talk to him about all kinds of things that the others just weren't interested in.

I knew that I understood Mr. Davenport better than anyone in the class, because I was going to be an artist when I grew up and he was particularly interested in art. He had been in Paris at the end of the war and had brought back some French art books that he loaned me now and then. I couldn't read the texts because they were in French, but I pored over the paintings for hours and tried to copy some of the artists' styles with my own paints at home. Then I would discuss the paintings with Mr. Davenport, and he always seemed very pleased that he had somebody to talk to who understood art as well as he did. He encouraged me to continue my studies in art, and I knew there was a special bond between us, even if he was eleven years older than I.

By the end of January I realized that I was spending a lot of my time either talking to Mr. Davenport or thinking of a reason to talk to him—or just thinking of him for no reason at all.

I studied art more feverishly than ever so we would have something to discuss. I learned that he liked poetry, so I dug up a copy of Robert Browning that someone had once given me. I had looked at it scornfully when I first got it and had never opened it. I had thought love poems were disgusting. Now I studied them carefully, trying to find an appropriate verse to discuss with Mr. Davenport.

My grandmother wondered why I was sitting around the house all the time, reading and "mooning about," as she called it, rather than going out with the girls. I couldn't explain it, but I just wanted to be alone. I stopped wearing jeans all the time and, for the first time in my life, worried about how my clothes looked. I stood in front of the mirror, wondering how I could look older.

My father threatened to take my favorite record and grind it up for fertilizer if I didn't stop playing it over and over. I told him he had no romance in his soul.

Chapter Two

BY EARLY FEBRUARY, only five weeks after I had first met Mr. Davenport, I realized that he had become the most important person in my life. My after-school chats with him were the highlights of my days, no matter how much teasing about being "teacher's pet" I had to take from the other kids. They didn't understand the real reason for my interest in him. I never discussed it with anyone, which was unusual for me because I usually said exactly what I thought about everything. This was different. I knew I had to keep it to myself.

One February afternoon I sat impatiently at my desk, watching Mr. Davenport write our English assignment on the blackboard. I wasn't paying much attention to what he was saying, because it was almost time to dismiss school for the day and I was rehearsing what I would say when I went up to his desk after class. I was returning one of the art books he had loaned to me, and I wanted to say something intelligent about the French Impressionists.

Instead of writing down the assignment, I was drawing a sketch of him in my notebook. My notebook was almost full of sketches of him and endless pages with his name written over and over in different styles of handwriting. I had never let anyone else see it. They could tease me about Billy Wild, but not about this.

The 3:30 bell finally rang, and I sat there, tightly clutching Mr. Davenport's book and waiting for everyone else to clear out so I could have a private talk with him. It was just my luck that everyone was hanging around in the classroom. Our big seventh-grade Valentine's Dance was the next week, and everybody was gossiping about it and buying tickets from the kids who were assigned to sell them.

Just as Carla Mae and Tanya came over to talk to me, I saw Mr. Davenport get up from his desk and head for the door.

"Mr. Davenport," I called, getting quickly out of my seat.

"Be right back, Addie," he said, and went out the door.

"Mr. Davenport, Mr. Davenport, sweetie," said Tanya in her ickiest voice, mocking me.

"Oh shut up, Smithers," I said.

"Don't tell me you're borrowing his books again!" said Carla Mae, grabbing at the art book. "You should get a library card from him!"

Sometimes I wondered why she was my best friend.

"Don't maul that book!" I said, grabbing it back from her. "This is a very rare volume, and practically irreplaceable!"

"Well, la-de-da!" said Tanya. "Why don't you hire a body-guard?"

"I wouldn't expect you to understand," I said. "You don't know anything about art."

"Ha!" Tanya said. "You're not half as interested in art as you are in Mr. Davenport."

"Yeah," said Carla Mae. "She's been slaving away for weeks creating the world's most gorgeous valentine for him."

"I have not!" I said hotly. "How do you know who I'm going to give it to?"

"Who else?" asked Tanya.

"Your other true love, Billy Wild!" said Carla Mae.

"Oh, you've gotta be kidding!" I said. "Yuck! I wouldn't give him the time of day . . . let alone a valentine."

"Oh, yeah?" said Carla Mae. "I bet you go to the Valentine's Dance with him."

"Yeah, you always go everywhere with him," said Tanya.

"Well who else is there in this dumb class?" I said, sounding disgusted. "I can't help it if he always asks me to everything."

"Oh come on," said Carla Mae. "After Mr. Davenport, Billy Wild is your second favorite."

"That's what you think!" I said. "I just may not go with him this time."

"Well, who else will you go with?" asked Tanya. "I hope you're not waiting for Mr. Davenport to ask you for a date!"

"Yeah," laughed Carla Mae. "You could wait forever! He's a bit old for you."

"I'm not waiting for anybody to ask me for a date!" I said. "And for your information, Mr. Davenport is only eleven years older than us. That's not so much. . . . When we graduate from high school we'll be eighteen, and he'll only be twenty-nine."

"Twenty-nine!" said Carla Mae. "Yuck! That's so old! I wouldn't want to go out with somebody who's an ancient twenty-nine!" I knew my father had been ten years older than my mother, and I closed my ears to Carla Mae's remarks. Though my mother had died a few months after I was born and I had never really known her, my grandmother had told me many times about the wonderful marriage my parents had. I had been thinking of the difference in their ages a lot lately when I thought of Mr. Davenport.

I longed to be grown up. Thirteen was such an awful age—
so clumsy. I knew I was no longer a child, but at thirteen people didn't treat me like a grown-up either. Some days I felt like
the kid I had always been, playing outdoors in jeans and sweat-
shirt, flinging myself into every game, my braids flying. Other
days I longed to be sophisticated, with beautiful clothes and
hair, and sit in elegant rooms and have serious conversations.

I never seemed to be able to look right. I hated my glasses but
had to wear them all the time. I knew I was too old for pigtails
but didn't quite know how else to do my hair. I suddenly felt
my clothes were wrong, and that my arms and legs were too
long for the rest of my skinny body. I hated being thirteen.

I wanted to be seventeen or eighteen so I could meet Mr.
Davenport on his own level and call him "Douglas" and go to
Omaha and have dinner with him in the Cottonwood Room at
the Blackstone Hotel and discuss the paintings in the Joslyn
Art Museum. Anything but be caught at the terrible in-between
age of thirteen. Even fourteen would have been better. After all,
Juliet had been fourteen, and Romeo took her seriously.

Just then I saw Billy Wild coming toward us, and Tanya and
Carla Mae giggled.

"Oh, here he comes, the Number Two in your life, Billy
Wild!" said Carla Mae when she saw him.

"Let's go," said Tanya. "The two lovebirds probably want to
be alone."

"Shut up, you guys!" I said.

As he came up to my desk, Tanya said, "Hi, Billy," in a high,
silly voice. Then she and Carla Mae giggled and headed for the
door.

Billy waited until they left.

"Going up to Cole's for a coke?" he asked.

"Maybe later," I said. "I have some things to do here first."

"I'll wait for you," he said.

"Don't bother," I said. "It might take me a while."

"That's OK," he said. "There's something I wanna ask you . . ."

"Listen," I interrupted, impatient that he wasn't getting the hint. "I have to talk to Mr. Davenport, and I'd like some privacy. So why don't you just go ahead without me?"

"What's so private between you and Davenport?" he asked, annoyed.

"None of your business!" I said.

"Well, how long is it going to take?" he asked.

"It's hard to say," I said, sounding mysterious. "So why don't you just run along?"

That made him angry.

"Well, why don't you stop making goo-goo eyes at Mr. Davenport?"

"That," I said cooly, "is a disgusting remark."

"Ooooo! Mr. Davenport," he said mockingly. "You're so cute!"

"Immature!" I said.

"Yeah," he said. "I know you like older men. . . ."

"I know five-year-olds who are more sophisticated and grown-up than you are!"

"Who wants to be an old man?" he said indignantly.

"Well, you could at least act your age!" I said. "We're in the seventh grade after all . . . that's practically high school!"

"Oh, could I help you across the street, old lady!" He smirked and grabbed my elbow.

"Adolescent ape!" I said, pulling my arm away. Angrily he turned and headed for the door.

I picked up my books and walked up to Mr. Davenport's desk to wait for him. I opened the art book to a painting I wanted to discuss with him, and as I was leafing through the book I heard someone writing on the blackboard behind me. I turned and saw that Billy had not left but was at the board, drawing a big heart in red chalk. Written inside was "Addie loves Mr. Davenport."

"You creep!" I said, and shot across the room to the blackboard.

Just then Mr. Davenport came back into the room. Billy took off, and I grabbed an eraser and lunged at the blackboard, frantically trying to erase the heart before Mr. Davenport saw it. He looked right at it and then turned quickly away. I was sure he had seen it.

"Finished with the book already?" he asked as I went back over to his desk.

"Yeah, for now," I said. "But I'd like to borrow it again sometime. I think the French Impressionists are my favorites."

"Mine, too," he said, smiling. "You'll have to take French when you get into high school. It will make studying the French painters a lot more interesting for you."

"I know. I'm dying to take French. But I wish I could just skip high school and go right on to college and get down to some serious things, you know?"

"I know how you feel," he said. "But you'll have a great time in high school. You don't want to miss all the fun."

I thought of how much fun it might be. I would be older, and a sophisticated high school student. I would come back and visit the seventh grade and see him. Things would be on a much more adult level between us then.

"Oh, it's all so childish," I said. "I just want to get started on my career . . . so I can go to Paris and study art."

"You'll have a terrific time," he said, and smiled at me.

That was one of the things I liked best about Mr. Davenport.

He took my dreams of being an artist as seriously as I did. Most grownups would laugh at them or patronize me—especially my dad, who thought my paintings were just some cute kids' phase I was going through. But my father didn't understand art well enough to see that I had talent. Mr. Davenport did. He knew about my sense of line and color and knew that I was good. He knew that I meant what I said; that I was really going to be an artist someday. Dad thought I would just be disappointed for aiming so high, but Mr. Davenport felt the way I did: you had to aim high to reach high.

"Of course you'll need to speak French when you live in Paris," he continued. "So I guess high school won't be a total waste for you, with French and art history."

I knew he was teasing me a bit, and I smiled.

"I hope we study a lot about the French Impressionists in high school art," I said. "That's how I'd like to paint when I go to Paris."

"Well, you may find a style of your own by then," he said. "You're very talented."

"Thanks," I said, blushing. I looked down at the book again. "Sometimes I get scared, though, when I look at these paintings —like some of the things Renoir did. I don't know if I'll ever be good enough. I mean to make a living being an artist."

"I think you will."

"I don't know. Sometimes I think maybe I should try something else. My dad says I should take typing and shorthand in high school, just in case . . ." That was typical of my dad, the combination of practicality and pessimism.

"That's OK, but you mustn't give up before you even get started," he said. "That's not like you, Addie."

I looked at him, trying to tell if he was just kidding me along, but I was sure he meant it. He knew me very well . . . maybe better than anybody.

"Well, I used to be more confident . . . about everything I guess, when I was just a kid. But when you grow up, you realize how scary things really are."

"Don't let other people's disappointments keep you from try-ing," he said, looking at me very carefully. "You'll regret it all your life if you do."

I wondered if Mr. Davenport was referring to my dad, but he couldn't have known him that well. Dad, who worked as a crane operator, had never finished high school and had always regretted it.

Mr. Davenport took out his plaid tobacco pouch and started filling his pipe. I had watched him do that dozens of times, and I knew that he smoked a wonderful tobacco mixture called "Rum and Maple." Whenever I thought of him, I could almost smell the wonderful scent of it. I had never had the courage to mention it to him before; it seemed so personal.

"I love the scent of that tobacco you smoke," I said as he lit his pipe. "What's the name of it?"

"Rum and Maple," he said, puffing away to get the pipe started.

I watched him intently. I thought he was more handsome than any movie star I had ever seen. I looked at the tobacco pouch lying on his desk.

"Do you think I could have just a little sample of that to give to my dad?" I asked suddenly. "I think he might like it. If he does, maybe I'll get him some for his birthday."

"Sure," he said, looking amused. "Your father smokes a pipe too, huh?"

I felt uneasy. My father never smoked a pipe, and I wondered if Mr. Davenport could know that.

"Well, he smokes one sometimes," I said hesitantly. "When he's not smoking cigarettes."

Mr. Davenport had taken a big pinch of tobacco out of the pouch.

"Here," he said. "How are you going to carry it?"

I quickly took out my neatly folded handkerchief, which Grandma insisted I carry with me every day, and spread it on his desk. He put the pinch of tobacco on it and I carefully rolled it up into the corner and tied it in a knot.

"Thanks," I said. "I bet my dad will love it."

"I hope so," he said. "Well, I have to get busy on these history papers, Addie, if you'll excuse me."

"OK," I said, reluctant to leave. "You're coming to the Valentine's Dance, aren't you?" I asked.

"Oh, sure," he said. "I wouldn't miss it. We used to have them when I was in grade school, too."

"Yeah, they're such kid stuff," I said. "I'd rather curl up at home with a good art book, but I guess we should all go since it's a class project."

"Of course," he said. "After all, they're crowning the King and Queen of Hearts. You don't want to miss that."

"Well, it's kind of silly," I said, trying to sound as blasé as possible. "Anyway, everyone knows it'll be Billy Wild and Carolyn Holt."

"I hope you'll be there," he said, and started shuffling the history papers around on the desk again.

I knew it was a signal that the conversation was over, but I hated to leave.

"Is there anything you want me to do around here?" I asked. "Put stuff away or something?"

He looked around. "No, nothing tonight, thanks," he said. "See you tomorrow."

"OK. *Au revoir*," I said.

He laughed. "*A bientôt*."

As I went out the door, I had a sudden moment of insight. I knew what had been the matter with me the last few weeks; something I thought would never happen to me in a million years. I was in love.

Chapter Three

OUR HOUSE WAS ONLY two blocks from the school, and I raced home through the biting cold February afternoon, carefully guarding the treasure tied up in my handkerchief. I went directly to the bedroom that Grandma and I shared and pulled the old bird's-eye maple dresser away from the wall to get at the keys hanging on the back. One of them unlocked my private drawer, the top left-hand drawer of the dresser. Grandma's private drawer was the top right-hand drawer, though she never locked it. Dad had a private drawer in his mahogany highboy, and he never locked his, either. I seemed to be the only one in the family with any real secrets.

Locks or not, it was an absolute rule that no one looked into anyone else's private drawer in our family. I knew my memento of Mr. Davenport would be safe there. What's more, I hoped it would scent all the things in my private drawer so that I would be reminded of him whenever I opened it. I hoped Dad and Grandma wouldn't notice if I began to smell like Rum and Maple. I closed my eyes and took a long, deep breath of the tobacco. I could see Mr. Davenport sitting at his desk, lighting up his pipe as we had one of our private talks. I carefully placed the knotted hanky in the drawer and locked it again.

I gathered up the red paper, lace doilies, ribbons and paints I had been making valentines with, and started for the kitchen. Our house wasn't very big. It had only two bedrooms, a kitchen, and a living room; and the kitchen was usually the center of activity. Grandma was almost always there, baking or canning or preparing something on her old cast-iron stove, and Dad and I just naturally gravitated to the good smells and coziness of the kitchen.

Dad had just come home from work and he was talking with Grandma. They didn't realize I was coming toward the kitchen, and I could overhear their conversation.

"She wants me to go to the dance, but I told her no," Dad was saying.

I couldn't imagine what dance he was talking about, or who would want him to go. He never went to dances. He was a quiet, reserved person who never went anywhere, in fact, except uptown for an occasional soft drink.

"Why not go?" asked Grandma.

"Well, I don't know—about Addie," he said.

"You're going to have to tell her sometime," said Grandma.

I stood very still, listening. I knew it was wrong to eavesdrop, but I couldn't have stopped if my life had depended on it.

"You know how Addie is," Dad said. "She's funny about people sometimes. I don't know how they'd get along."

"Irene Davis is a nice woman," said Grandma. "I think they oughta meet."

I froze. I couldn't believe it. Irene Davis! I thought I knew everything there was to know about Dad. I never imagined he had any private life other than the one he shared with us. He had never dated anyone since my mother had died twelve years ago. And Irene Davis of all people!

Irene ran one of the two beauty salons in Clear River. She had been widowed several years ago when her husband had been killed in an accident in the railroad yards, and she lived alone, operating her beauty salon out of an extra room in her house.

She was in her early forties, tall and blond and very good looking, if you liked the obviously glamorous type. I thought she was a bit too done-up for a little Nebraska town like Clear River, but I guess she thought her high heels, bright red nail polish and swept-up blond hair were good advertising for her salon.

Irene played the organ for the Methodist church on Sundays, and, though most people thought she was very talented, some of the more conservative members claimed she put too much rhythm into the hymns. My family went to the Baptist church, so I had never heard her Sunday performances; but I had heard her play at a couple of wedding ceremonies, and I thought "Here Comes the Bride" did sound kind of jazzy the way she did it.

She was always laughing and talking and obviously having a good time wherever she went, and sometimes I would see her at the bar in the back room of Cole's Confectionery, having a beer with a group of people. There was something just a little too bold about her that scared me in some way. Nobody in my family ever behaved that way, and I wasn't sure how to react. But to imagine her with my dad, with his stern, quiet manner, was simply crazy. It must be some kind of mistake. I had to find out more about it.

I couldn't stand there listening any longer, so I went into the kitchen with my armload of valentine makings and pretended that I hadn't heard anything but the last remark.

"Who ought to meet whom?" I asked as I plopped down at the table with all my stuff.

"Oh, nothing," said Dad, looking uncomfortable. "Just talking about some folks we know."

"Don't get all settled there," said Grandma. "Dinner's almost ready, and you'd better set the table."

"In a minute," I said impatiently. "Who were you talking about?" I asked Dad again. I was enjoying putting him on the spot. It seemed we did that to each other a lot; sometimes in fun, sometimes to see who would get the upper hand. We had always had a talent for annoying each other, but now that I was growing up I was getting better at holding up my end of the struggle. Dad seemed more and more confused about how to deal with me as I got older, and I soon learned that his puzzlement was my best weapon. In spite of all the sparring, however, Dad and I liked each other a lot.

"You just tend to your own business," he said.

"Well, what's going on?" I asked.

"Now, Addie," said Grandma. "You mustn't butt into other people's business when they don't want to discuss it."

Actually Grandma would be the first to confide something like this if she could do it without making Dad angry.

"My gosh!" I said. "We're in the same family aren't we? What the heck's the big secret?"

"I don't butt into your private business, do I?" asked Dad. "I don't read your diary. I don't ask who those mushy valentines you're making are for, do I?"

"These are not mushy!" I said. One of them was kind of special, though, and I quickly covered it up so he wouldn't see it. It was for Mr. Davenport. The other valentines were for Dad and Grandma and Carla Mae and a few of the other kids I especially liked.

"I'll bet the sweetest valentine is for Billy Wild," said

Grandma, teasing me. I knew she was helping Dad change the subject.

"It is not!" I said hotly. "Yuck! I can't stand him. You should see the way he behaves—like a three-year-old."

I busied myself with the cutting and pasting of lace doilies over the red construction paper. I was trying to think of a way to find out more about Irene.

"I wish we had a telephone," I said to no one in particular. I said that often, but Dad never would spend the money for a phone.

"So Billy Wild could call you?" he asked.

"No!" I said. "Honestly, I don't know where you two get the mistaken idea that I like him! Nobody could be that desperate!"

Actually he was right on target. I would have to go to the dance with somebody, and it might as well be Billy Wild.

"Huh!" said Dad.

"I mean we should have a phone so anybody could call us," I said. "Or like for an emergency or something."

"Like talking to boys, I suppose," said Dad.

"No!"

"No use havin' a phone," said Grandma. "It's just a nuisance. It rings and you just have to run and answer it."

Grandma always said that when I suggested a phone, and I had tried forever to make her see that answering the phone when it rang was the whole point, but she just refused to understand. Grandma was in her seventies, and she had been around long enough to have her own way of looking at things. She seldom changed those ways, either.

"Well, like I always say," said Dad, "if anybody wants to talk to us . . ."

"I know, I know," I interrupted glumly, finishing the sentence with him. "They can write us a letter or knock on the door."

"That's right!" he said with an air of finality.

"My gosh!" I said. "We're the only people in this whole town without a telephone. We're living in the eighteenth century! It's a miracle we have indoor plumbing around here!"

"You just be thankful we do," said Dad. "I sure didn't have it when I was a boy!"

"Well, this is 1949!" I said, exasperated. "The telephone is a miracle of modern communication, and we should participate in it!"

"You can put in a miracle whenever you can pay for it," he said.

Money was usually the end of every conversation with Dad. Our house was comfortable, but very plain, and there wasn't an object in it that could have been referred to as a luxury.

Suddenly I had an idea how to get the conversation rerouted toward Irene again.

"Speaking of money," I said. "I gotta have a new dress and a pair of high heels for the Valentine's Dance next week."

"What?" said Dad, sounding shocked. "High heels? You don't wear high heels!"

"Well, I'm going to!" I said. "The girls are all going to get them for this dance . . . it'll be the inauguration for all of us."

"Inauguration?" he said.

"For wearing high heels the first time!"

"You're too young for that!" he said.

"I am not! I'm thirteen! I can't go to the dance looking like a five-year-old!"

"She's right, James," said Grandma. "I talked to Mrs. Carter the other day, and she said Carla Mae and all the girls are going to wear their first high heels to the dance."

"See?" I said to him. "And I need a new party dress."

"Oh, boy," he said. "There goes another twenty dollars."

"Well, I'm not going looking like an eighteenth century farm maid, even if they did do that when you were a boy."

He glared at me. "I was born in the twentieth century, too, you know," he said.

Then I moved in with my idea.

"And I ought to get a permanent, too," I said, watching Dad closely.

"A permanent!" he said, giving me a sharp look. "Since when did you ever need a permanent? You've never had one in your life—haven't been able to drag you near a beauty parlor for thirteen years!"

"That was when I was little!" I said.

"She oughta have one if she's goin' to the dance in a fancy dress and high heels," said Grandma.

"Yeah," I said, warming up to the idea. "I can't go in pigtails! It's not sophisticated." That was a bonus I hadn't even thought of. A permanent would make me look older.

"Sophisticated!" he snorted. "Huh! Don't know why anybody who spends half her time playing baseball and basketball would worry about being sophisticated!"

"I don't do that!" I said. In fact, I always had played baseball and basketball and every other sport available. But recently most of the girls had begun to lose interest for some reason, and my only choice was to give it up or play with the boys and take the teasing that went with it.

"Every other girl in our class got a permanent centuries ago," I went on. "Carla Mae gets one every year. Think of all the money I've been saving you for thirteen years."

"You don't have to do it just because everyone else does," he said. "Grandma can curl your hair with the curling iron. She always did when you were little."

"Oh, that won't do," said Grandma, smiling. "She wants to look her best for Billy."

"Oh, my gosh! I told you I don't even like him!"

"Did he invite you to the dance?" she asked.

"No," I said, sounding disgusted, "but he's going to. I suppose I'll have to go with him too; there's nobody else worth going with in that dumb bunch."

"Well, you'd better make an appointment for your permanent pretty soon," said Grandma.

"Yeah," I said casually, watching Dad out of the corner of my eye. "I'll go see Irene Davis tomorrow."

"Irene Davis?" said Dad, looking at Grandma. "I thought Grandma always went to Mrs. Jacobsen."

"Oh, she does all the older ladies' hair," I said. "Irene is more stylish. All the girls go to her."

Grandma was looking over at me to see if I was up to something. She was almost always able to tell, but I kept an absolutely straight face and didn't let on a thing. She could usually read my mind, but this time she wasn't quite sure. However, I could see that she was all for the idea of my going to see Irene.

She smiled. "You better get your appointment tomorrow, Addie," she said, "before Irene gets busy with the other girls."

"Right," I said. "I'll do that."

Grandma looked very pleased, and Dad looked more uncomfortable than ever.

Chapter Four

THE NEXT AFTERNOON we were at Cole's Confectionery, our after-school hangout on Main Street. Cole's had a big soda-fountain area, with booths and tables up front, and a bar in the back room where the grownups would stop for a beer. A lot of working men came in on the way home; sometimes farmers in overalls stopped by, and couples would come in later after dinner. But the front room of Cole's was the kids' territory, and we made the most of it.

Carla Mae and I and three other girls were all crammed into one booth. The table was loaded with everything from candy bars to lime sodas to potato chips to my favorite Cole's "Dime Sundae"—a scoop of chocolate ice cream with butterscotch sauce—which we all shared. When the waitress wasn't looking, we wet the tips of the covers of our paper straws and blew them at the ceiling, trying to get them to stick there. When they dried enough, they would flutter down, hopefully in someone's beer or ice cream, which would send us into shrieks of triumph.

Several boys were over at the pinball machine in the corner, making hoots of noise as usual, and looking over to see if we noticed how neat they were.

We were talking about what we were going to wear to the dance and who was going with whom and who would be elected King and Queen. I hated to see Billy Wild get the satisfaction of being elected, but everyone thought he would.

"If you think he's vain now," I said, "just wait!"

"Well, he is cute," said Carla Mae. "And you know it."

"He knows it, too," I said. "He'll probably wear his crown to class for the rest of the year."

We all giggled.

"Speak of the devil," said Carla Mae.

We looked over and saw Billy coming in the door with Tanya. He joined the other boys at the pinball machine and made a big show of pounding on the sides until it tilted and shut off.

"Oh, look at him!" I said, disgusted. "He is so obnoxious!"

"Yeah?" said one of the other girls. "Then how come you're always talking about him?"

"That's just to cover up for her real love," laughed Carla Mae. "Mr. Davenport!"

"Oh shut up, Carter!" I said, embarrassed.

Carla Mae suddenly grabbed my notebook and whipped open the cover where Mr. Davenport's first name was written in several different styles.

"See!" Carla Mae said triumphantly. "She just keeps writing his name over and over." They all laughed.

"I wasn't writing his name!" I said. "I was just practicing different kinds of handwriting. I was just using the name Douglas . . ."

I knew they wouldn't let me get away with that. They kept laughing, and I tried to grab the notebook back from them. As we were tussling and squirming around in the booth, Billy threw a piece of ice at us.

"Disgusting!" shouted Carla Mae.

"Oh, yuck!" I said. "He is so immature! And I suppose I have to go to the dance with that!"

"Oh, I can tell it's just killing you," said Carla Mae, sarcastically. "Has he asked you yet?"

"No, I'm not speaking to him at the moment," I said. "He'll just have to wait."

Tanya came over, and as she squeezed into the booth with us Billy gave a loud wolf whistle.

"Creep!" I said.

"Oh, she hates him so much!" said Carla Mae, mocking me.

"Well," said Tanya, "I'm glad you can't stand him any more and don't want to go to the dance with him."

"Why?" I asked.

"Because he just asked me to go, and I said yes," she answered.

Everybody else was very quiet. I froze. I couldn't think of a thing to say.

I felt humiliated, but I didn't know why. I didn't even *like* Billy. Darn him anyway. I would look ridiculous going to the dance alone. He had really thrown a kink in my plans. And asking Tanya instead of me was the final insult. He didn't even like her! At least he had never shown any interest in her before. I figured he must be trying to get even with me for giving him the brush-off after school the day before. But this was going too far. He couldn't really like Tanya more than me. I wondered. But why did I care what Billy thought?

I walked home from Cole's feeling dumb and angry. That stupid Billy had let me sit around all that time thinking he was going to invite me and then had invited Tanya instead. I couldn't believe it.

I wandered into the kitchen where Grandma was ironing and sat down glumly at the table. She looked over at me.

"Not even a hello for your own grandmother?" she asked, smiling.

"Hello," I said, grim.

"Glory!" she said. "Could mop the floor with your chin all the way down there."

I just sighed.

"You'd better get the table set. Your dad will be home for supper soon."

"What's going on with him, anyway?" I asked, not wanting to reveal my eavesdropping about Irene.

Grandma looked as though she were going to say something and then thought better of it.

"Well, you'll find out in good time," she said.

"Nobody ever tells me anything around here!" I said angrily. I would find out for myself if they were going to be that way about it.

I got up and got plates and silverware and listlessly dumped them around at our three places on the table.

Grandma was watching me. She could always tell when something was wrong. She seemed to know me much better than Dad did. Grandma had come to live with us when my mother had died more than twelve years ago, and the three of us had been a family ever since. Some people thought it was an unusual situation—my being raised by my grandmother—but I was so young when my mother died that I didn't remember her at all, and having Grandma there seemed quite natural and ordinary to me.

Yet Grandma herself was anything but ordinary. She was, in fact, a bit of a character. She always worked around the house in an old faded cotton housedress, Indian moccasins and an apron made from an even older, cut-down cotton dress. When she was doing heavy cleaning she would put a "dust-cap," a little ruffled cotton cap, over her hair, and she looked as I imagined David Copperfield's Aunt Betsy had.

Grandma was short and shapeless with age, but she had fantastic energy and whizzed around the house with a terrific clatter, which sometimes annoyed my dad. It wasn't easy for a grown man to be living with his own mother—especially Grandma, who was not intimidated by anyone—but they managed to get along pretty well.

One reason for the relatively peaceful existence at our house was that Grandma was as sensitive as she was strong-willed. She could always tell when my dad and I were about to annoy each other to the point of an explosion, and by now she was an expert at defusing us.

She was also an expert at finding out what was on my mind when I had no intention of talking about it. I finished setting the table and slumped down in my chair.

"Bad day at school today?" she asked.

"No."

She kept prodding around till we got on the subject of Billy, and then the whole story came out about his asking Tanya.

"Well, I'm not too surprised," said Grandma. "The way you treat Billy. You're not very nice to him sometimes, and he acts like he's real sweet on you . . ."

"Oh, what does he know? He's so immature!" I said. "I wouldn't have gone with him if he had asked me, that creep!"

"He's not as grown-up as your Mr. Davenport, is that it?" she asked.

"Who said anything about Mr. Davenport?"

"I don't know . . . I hear his name an awful lot around here."

"Well, I just wish I was older, that's all," I said angrily. "If I was just four years older . . . I'd be seventeen . . . I could do what I want and date grown-up people and . . . I could even get married if I was seventeen."

"Married!" said Grandma. "First time I ever heard talk of that. Thought you was goin' to Paris and study art and never get married."

"Oh, you know what I mean!" I said, exasperated. "I just want to be old enough to do what I want."

"Well, just be sure you *know* what you want," said Grandma.

"I do!"

"I don't know . . ." she said. "Sounds like you wanted Billy to ask you to the dance, and then sounds like you didn't care one way or the other."

"Well, I don't want to be the only one there without a date!"

"Now, Addie, that's not a good reason for going out with somebody, just so you'll have a date. That's using somebody. It ain't right. You shouldn't go unless you like the fella."

"Oh, well, I like him well enough to go to a dance with him, I guess," I said. I didn't want to think about Billy. I was worried about my own problems, but I couldn't help thinking about what Grandma had said. I had been so busy thinking about going to the dance and making an impression on Mr. Davenport that I hadn't considered Billy's feelings. If he really did like me he must have been hurt by my refusal to take him seriously.

I put that thought aside. It seemed like a whole new complicated set of ideas that I didn't want to bother with at the moment; but I was left with the nagging feeling that I had not been very nice to Billy, and that it was all my fault that he was going with Tanya.

"I don't even think I'll go to the dumb dance," I said.

"Your dad already paid for your ticket, didn't he?" Grandma asked.

"Yeah. I think I'll just throw it away."

"He'll have a fit if you waste a fifty-cent ticket," she said.

"I'm not going by myself!" I said angrily.

"Well, ask someone then," she said.

"Oh, Grandma, I can't do that!" I said. "Girls don't do the asking. I'd be a laughing stock. It's so unfair! Girls just have to sit and wait."

"Well, sometimes it's hard for boys, too," Grandma said. "Always havin' to be the first one to show how they feel— always havin' to do the asking, wondering if the girl's going to turn them down. Sometimes a girl needs to show she likes a boy, too—to help him out a little. And there's nothing wrong in that, so long as she really means it."

I knew Grandma was talking about Billy, but I wasn't thinking about him at all. I was thinking about Mr. Davenport and what I could do to show him how much I cared about him. Maybe if I made the first move in some way, he would think of me as more than just a student. I would have to impress him at the dance. I would have to look older and more sophisticated— a serious person with whom he could share his life.

"Well, what if you show you like someone," I asked, "and he doesn't like you back?"

"That's a chance everyone has to take," she said. "You'll find the right person one of these days; you'll see."

"How do you know?" I asked. "How do you know when it's the right person? And how do you know where he is? What if he's in Paris or Rome or somewhere, not here in Clear River? How are you supposed to find somebody?"

"Things have a way of working themselves out."

"Oh, you always say stuff like that!" I said, exasperated. "It just doesn't make any sense. When you find somebody, then he doesn't even like you back, so what's the use?"

"You'll find somebody to like you back sooner or later."

"That's easy for you to say. You fell in love with Grandpa, and he fell in love with you, and there it was—all settled."

"It wasn't quite that easy," she said. "I had my share of disappointments, too, before I settled down."

I had never heard Grandma say anything like that before, and I looked up at her, curious.

"What do you mean?" I asked.

"Well, Grandpa wasn't quite what I would have planned for myself if I coulda had everything just my way," she said.

"Why not?"

"There was somebody else I liked a lot, too."

That amazed me. I had never thought of Grandma as having cared about any man but Grandpa.

"You mean you didn't just meet him and say, 'That's Mr. Right'?"

"Well, not quite."

"What happened?"

"Well, when I was about sixteen my folks sent me to Des Moines to help out our Aunt Lizzie. She was ill and needed someone to help nurse her. I stayed there almost eighteen months, and while I was there I met Grandpa. We both sang in the church choir, and he was a real nice young man. We began to see each other, and after a while we got engaged.

"When Aunt Lizzie passed on, I had to come back to my folks here, and Grandpa promised to sell his land in Des Moines and come out here and find a farm, and we'd be married. I had to wait for him for several months until he could arrange every-

thing, and I started seeing an old school chum of mine named Tom Childers. Before I knew what happened, I was head over heels in love with Tom."

I was amazed. "Really?" I asked.

"I guess I never knew what it felt like before," said Grandma. "I thought the affection I felt for your grandpa was the best thing one could hope for. When I met Tom, I knew different.

"But your grandpa was selling his land and was on his way to Nebraska to marry me, and in those days—you know it was the 1890s—well, you just didn't back down on an engagement after a man made that kind of promise to you. So I stopped seeing Tom, and when your grandpa arrived here, I never let on a thing, and I went ahead and married him."

"You mean you married somebody you didn't love and gave up the right person?" I asked, incredulous.

"Well," Grandma said thoughtfully, "I don't know as there's any one 'right person' for anybody. After Grandpa and I were married, I grew to love him. He was a fine man and a good husband, and I don't think I coulda loved Tom any more than I did your grandpa after forty years of marriage. Who's to say?"

"But whatever happened to Tom?" I asked.

"Oh, he moved away, and years later I heard he was married and had a family. I'm sure he was happy, too. I think there's more than one person you could be happy with. You just have to choose the best you can and try and make it work. You'll see; you'll find somebody one of these days."

I thought about that for a moment and tried to imagine if Mr. Davenport might be the right person.

"Dad was ten years older than my mother, wasn't he?" I asked.

"Yes," said Grandma.

"Did he think she was just a kid at first?"

"Well, she was eighteen when they met, and out of high school," Grandma answered.

I wondered if Mr. Davenport would wait five years for me until I was older and out of high school. It all seemed hopeless.

"I'm not going to the dance alone!" I said again.

"Now, Addie," said Grandma. "Some of the other boys are bound to ask you."

"What if they don't?"

"Of course they will," she said. "And you'll have your new dress and new shoes, and you'll get your permanent. Why you'll look fine."

Chapter Five

I DRAGGED MYSELF OUT of the house the afternoon before the dance to go over to Irene Davis's Beauty Salon. Grandma nearly had to push me out the door, because getting myself all fixed up was the last thing I wanted to do. As far as I could tell, there wasn't anybody left in the class who didn't have a date, and I would feel like a creep going to the dance alone. I didn't know why I was bothering with a permanent. At the same time, I was terribly curious about Irene, and I finally agreed to go because I wanted to get a closer look at her.

I was moping along the sidewalk staring at the scuffed toes of my saddle shoes when I heard a car horn toot just behind me. I looked around and there he was. Mr. Davenport was pulling up beside me in his neat, tan Chevrolet convertible. He rolled down the window and leaned across the front seat.

"Hi, Addie."

"Hi, Mr. Davenport!" I said, wishing I had worn my good coat and hat.

"Can I give you a lift anywhere?" he asked. "It's freezing!"

"Yeah, thanks," I said, and got into the car. He had stopped to give us kids a lift before, but this was the first time I had ever been alone in the car with him. If only I had met him coming home from Irene's when I looked better.

"Which way are you going?" he asked.

"I'm just going over to Irene Davis's to have my hair done," I said, trying to sound as though I did it every day.

He smiled.

"Getting ready for the big night?"

"What big night?" I asked, trying to be blasé.

"The Valentine's Dance!" he laughed.

"Oh," I said. "That! It's all so childish."

"It'll be fun," he said.

"I don't even know if I want to go," I said. "I might just drop by for a little while and see what's happening."

"Well, there's a reason I want you to be there," he said, looking over at me.

"What?" I asked.

"I'll tell you at the dance," he said, and smiled.

I smiled back at him, trying to be casual, but my heart nearly stopped. What could he want to tell me? It had to be something special—something he was saving for an occasion like the Valentine's Dance. Maybe he had finally realized that I was much more mature than my thirteen years, and we would have a heart–to–heart talk. I felt almost as though he had asked me for a date.

We pulled up in front of Irene's house, and I jumped out.

"Well, see you at the dance," I said.

"Right," he said, and drove off, waving to me as he turned the corner.

I was so elated over this new turn of events in my relationship with Mr. Davenport that I almost forgot why I had come to

Irene's that afternoon. As I knocked on the door, I was busy daydreaming about what a new hair-do was going to do for me. It would make me look a lot older—with any luck at least sixteen. And with that and my high heels and new dress, Mr. Davenport couldn't help but be impressed.

Suddenly Irene opened the door, and my fantasy evaporated. There she was in her pink smock, swept-up blond hair and open-toed wedgies, with bright red toenails poking out. I could not believe that my father would have anything to do with this woman.

"Hi, Addie," she said in a friendly tone of voice.

I had never been to her salon before, but she knew me because Clear River was such a small town that most of the 1,500 people knew the other 1,499.

I returned her greeting, feeling a little uncomfortable. I had to find out more about her, but I wasn't sure how to go about it.

"I was sure surprised when you made an appointment," she said. "You've never been in before."

"Oh, I've never even had a permanent before," I said. "But we've got a big Valentine's Dance tomorrow, and I wanted my hair to look different."

"I'll be at that dance," said Irene. "I'm gonna play the piano for the King and Queen ceremony."

I looked over at her. Could that have been the dance she wanted my father to go to? I hoped she wouldn't jazz up the music too much and ruin the dance.

"How's your grandma?" she asked.

"Oh, she's fine."

"And your dad?"

"Fine," I said tensely. I was supposed to find out about her, and she was giving me the third degree.

"Did your dad suggest you come over here for a permanent?"

I looked startled. What a question! That showed how little she knew about my father!

"Gosh, no!" I said. "He doesn't even want me to have a permanent. He thinks they're stupid!" That would stop her.

Irene gave me an odd look in the mirror.

"Well, you know how men are," she said cheerfully. "They don't know anything about what it takes for us to look glamorous."

I didn't like her including me in that "us." I had no intention of ever looking anything like her.

She motioned me to a chair in front of the mirror, and I plopped down and looked around the room as she got her equipment together. There were a couple of big, silver, bullet-shaped hair dryers on one wall, a shampoo sink with a mirror over it, several mismatched chairs, and a coffee table covered with movie magazines. There were photos of swanky, movie-star hair-dos on the wall, and a little rolling table which held every imaginable color of nail polish. Over in one corner was an evil-looking electric permanent machine with wires and clamps dangling from it. I eyed it with some misgivings. On the counter in front of me was a garish, gold-plated trophy of a Greek goddess with wings. I inspected it closely. It was engraved "Mrs. Irene Davis, Third Prize Hair Styling, Nebraska State Cosmetologists Convention, 1947."

I was a little relieved to see that. At least she had some talent. I thought again about how glamorous I would look when she finished.

Irene unbraided my hair and brushed it out.

"My, you sure got pretty hair, Addie."

"Thank you," I said, watching her every move carefully in the mirror.

"Well, we're gonna fix you up real fine for the big dance. Let's see if we can find a style you'd like."

She brought over a huge hairstyle book, and as the two of us leafed through it she discussed the merits of some of the various hair-dos.

"Rita Hayworth wore that in her last film," she said about one glamorous, swept-up style.

I glanced up at Irene in the mirror and saw that it was almost like her own.

"No," I said distastefully. "That's too overdone."

Irene laughed.

"Yeah," she said. "I guess it's too much for somebody your age."

Her remark annoyed me. I hoped she didn't think I was just a kid.

"Well, I do want something that will make me look older," I said worriedly.

She smiled.

"Not too old," she said. "I think we can come up with something you'll like—something that looks like you but just a little more sophisticated."

"Yeah," I said happily. "Exactly."

She moved me over to the shampoo sink and tilted my chair back and started washing my hair.

"So how do you like being in the seventh grade?" she asked.

"OK," I said, squinting to keep the soap out of my eyes.

"You've got that Mr. Davenport for a teacher, huh?"

"Yeah," I said.

"He's a cute one, huh?" she said.

"Yeah," I said. I thought it was disgusting! Calling a grown man like Mr. Davenport "cute." Billy Wild might be "cute," but Mr. Davenport was handsome.

"Like having a man teacher for a change?"

"Yeah," I said again. I suddenly wondered if Dad had said something about me to her, or if he knew about my feelings for Mr. Davenport. Then I thought it was unlikely. I had never mentioned it to him, and even though Grandma had caught on, I doubted that she told Dad.

"Is he a good teacher?" Irene asked.

"Oh, sure, he's great!" I said enthusiastically. Then I realized again she was finding out more and more about me, and I hadn't been getting anywhere with my investigation of her.

"How long have you been in business?" I blurted out.

"Me?" she said, surprised. "Oh, about six or seven years now. Let's see—seven years in April! Golly, it doesn't seem that long to me."

She rinsed my hair and sat me upright again.

"You don't want a manicure, do you?" she asked.

I looked at my hands and quickly hid them under the apron she had draped over me. I would need to do something about my nails before seeing Mr. Davenport at the dance, but I would do it myself. I didn't want Irene to see what my hands looked like from playing basketball in gym class and messing around in my paints.

Anyway, I thought all that stuff about make-up and manicures was a little confusing, and I didn't want Irene to know how ignorant I was. The other girls' mothers helped them with such things, but Grandma wasn't up on the latest styles, and I had to be more observant than most girls to learn how to put myself together.

I watched as Irene put lotion and curlers on my hair and wound each one tightly to my scalp. She was very intense about it and seemed to be concentrating very hard.

"How can you stand to do this over and over all day long?"
I asked. "Don't you get bored?"

She gave me a surprised look in the mirror. "Gosh, no!" she
said. "I think it's real creative, trying to help all different kinds
of people look their best."

"I never thought of it that way," I said.

"Well, it's just like any other job," she went on. "You get
out of it just what you put into it. If you're enthusiastic, then
people like you and like what you do, and you have a good time,
and it's just that simple."

Her enthusiasm numbed me, and I couldn't think of a thing
to say.

"You remember to tell your grandma hello from me," Irene
said. "I always thought she was such a fine person. She's sure
done a wonderful job of raising you since your momma died."

I was going to reply, but Irene rattled on.

"Course a girl your age would like to have a younger woman
around once in a while I suppose, to help with clothes and
make-up and hair and all that . . ."

She was watching me in the mirror as she said that, and
I wondered how she knew what I had been thinking a few
moments before. She couldn't have guessed; she was just making a brazen hint. I wondered if she had tried to use that line on
my dad.

"No," I said, very cool. "Grandma's done very well by me. I
don't think it matters what age she is."

"Well, that's a wonderful thing to say," Irene said, but she
didn't sound particularly convinced.

I tried once more to launch my investigation.

"What do you do in your spare time?" I asked. "You have
any hobbies or anything?"

She looked a bit surprised at the question. "Me?" she said. "Oh, gosh . . . nothing special. I bowl once a week, and I love to dance," she laughed. "Like to kick up my heels."

I gave her a disgusted look which she couldn't see.

Then she did what I was dreading. She moved me over by the electric permanent machine.

"So you do the permanent on this?" I asked apprehensively.

"Yep, this is the monster," she said, laughing. "We hook you up and plug you right in."

"You have any special training for this?" I asked. "A license or anything?"

"Just beauty school," she said.

"Looks like it would burn your head off," I said nervously.

"Haven't lost a customer yet," Irene said cheerfully, and started hooking one of the machine's metal clamps to each curler on my head.

She turned on the machine, gave me a pat on the shoulder, shoved a movie magazine into my hands, and went on about her work across the room.

I sat there stiff as a board, expecting to be electrocuted any minute and wondering if the result was going to be worth all this trouble.

Chapter Six

THE AFTERNOON OF THE VALENTINE'S DANCE I must have changed my mind twenty or thirty times about whether I was going. One minute I imagined how glamorous I'd be—sweeping into the gymnasium in my new dress and high heels. Everyone would marvel at how much older and more mature I looked. Mr. Davenport would look at me and smile and ask me to dance and tell me what he had been waiting to tell me all this time.

The next minute I saw myself slouching into the gym all alone, with everyone whispering and glancing at the only wallflower there without a date. My dress and shoes and hair would look all wrong, and Mr. Davenport would have to struggle not to laugh when he saw me trying to be grown-up.

I kept hoping I would suddenly come down with the flu or measles or something so the decision would be taken out of my hands, but I was disgustingly healthy.

Grandma, who had a strong stubborn streak and a very direct way of dealing with any opposition, was having none of my indecision. She forced me into a kitchen chair that afternoon and wet my newly permanented hair and rolled it up in rag curlers. I jiggled and jerked around in my chair.

"Hold still," Grandma said. "You're nervous as a cat in a room full of rockin' chairs."

I laughed in spite of myself. Grandma knew her old country expressions always tickled me, and she would dredge them up at crucial moments to relieve the tension. I would always try to think of one to answer with, and then it would become a game as we batted them back and forth. She almost always won.

"Steady as a rock," I said, holding out my hands.

"Shakin' like a leaf," she answered.

"Cool as a cucumber," I said.

"Hotter than a two-dollar pistol," she said, hand on my forehead.

"Calm as a—uh—calm as a . . . a . . . clam!" I said.

"That ain't a sayin'!" she laughed.

"Yes it is!"

"Never heard of it," she said.

"I just made it up!" I said.

"Don't count!" said Grandma.

"Oh, phooey!" I said irritably. "Aren't you finished?"

"Addie," she said quietly. "Just calm down. Everything's going to go just fine."

I wanted to believe her.

I ran around with my hair in curlers for the rest of the afternoon, helping Grandma put the finishing touches on my dress and making sure her best rhinestone bracelet looked OK with it. My dress was a pale pink taffeta. It was very chic and understated, I thought, and made me look very mature. In my more positive moments, I expected everyone at the dance would comment on how I had aged, seemingly overnight.

After dinner, I started my final preparations. I put on my best white slip, a new pair of nylon stockings, and my hated garter belt.

As far as I could tell, garter belts had been invented by the same people who had thought up medieval torture instruments. My garter belt was a disgusting, flesh-colored satin, and fastened about the waist with hooks and eyes in the back. Since you could never hope to fasten hooks and eyes without seeing them, you had to put the garter belt on backwards, hook it over your stomach, and then wrestle it around so that the hooks were in the back.

That left three long strips of elastic dangling down each leg, to fasten your stockings to. Each strip of elastic had a pink rubber knob and metal clamp on the end. The trick was to capture the top of your nylon stocking over the pink knob and then press the knob into the metal clamp before the stocking slipped off the knob or the elastic slipped out of your hand and snapped up and hit you in the face.

To add to the confusion, the strips of elastic were adjustable up and down, and there were three different lengths of stockings you could buy. So you had to work out the right combination of stocking length and elastic adjustment for your particular legs or else your stocking would droop down around your ankles like elephant skin, or they would be held so taut by a too-short elastic that you would have to walk all bent over like the hunchback of Notre Dame.

If that wasn't enough, you also had to worry about the seams in the back of your stockings being straight up and down. In order to do that, you had to see the back of your entire leg from ankle to thigh all at the same time while holding your leg straight and simultaneously keeping a firm grasp on the rear elastic strip of your garter belt with one hand and a firm grasp on your stocking top with the other hand. There was, obviously, no way in the world anyone could do all of that at the same time. I hated garter belts.

After a lot of wrestling with the stockings, the seams appeared fairly straight, and I pulled on my old chenille bathrobe and started putting on make-up. It would be the first time I had ever worn any in public, though we practiced using it at slumber parties.

I stood in front of the bedroom mirror, squinting a bit to see without my glasses. Grandma watched closely at my elbow, and Dad stood in the doorway looking apprehensive.

"Thought they didn't wear war paint until high school," he said.

"Well, this is a special occasion," Grandma answered.

I was concentrating hard, trying to pat some of Grandma's loose powder on my face and raising a cloud of powder dust that nearly choked me. When the air cleared, Grandma handed me a hanky and suggested I wipe off a bit of it.

Then I used some of her cream rouge to color my cheeks a bit, and she watched closely to see that I didn't use too much and look like a "painted woman."

The next step was lipstick—a brand new tube of "Ruby Red" I had bought at the Clear River Pharmacy that morning.

I started coloring in my lips very carefully, rolling them around over my teeth as I had seen women do, trying to draw a straight line.

"Looks a little heavy on the left side to me," Dad said.

"Not through yet," I said, mumbling through my facial contortions.

I was twisting this way and that, trying to see, almost holding my head upside down. "The light in here is awful!" I said irritably.

"Try not to get any on your teeth," Grandma said helpfully.

"Can't do it if you talk to me!" I said, annoyed.

I finished and mushed my lips around together to even out the color, then made a big puckery mouth at myself in the mirror.

"Oh, boy!" said Dad. "I can't take any more." He turned and left the room.

I stood there silently, surveying myself in the mirror. It was hard to tell what the final result would be; I was still in bathrobe and curlers. Grandma was watching me in the mirror.

"Am I pretty?" I asked, turning to her suddenly.

She looked at me quietly for a moment, as though she were thinking of an answer.

"Well, am I?" I said, almost angry. "I just want to know!"

"Why I think you're as good lookin' as any girl could hope to be," Grandma said.

"That's not what I mean!"

"Well, everybody's got their own ideas of what's pretty and what ain't. You're sure pretty-lookin' to me."

"Oh, that's just because you know me!" I said, angry.

Grandma put her hands on my shoulders and turned me to face her.

"Addie," she said seriously. "You are pretty. You're as pretty as any girl ever needs to be."

I looked back at her for a long moment, not convinced that I was going to be pretty enough to impress Mr. Davenport.

"Come on now," said Grandma. "Put your shoes on and come out in the kitchen so I can comb out your hair."

I listlessly poked my feet into my new high heels. They were

stiff leather pumps, and on my way to the kitchen I discovered
that they required more than a casual practice run. I couldn't
resist clowning and walking on the sides of my ankles in them.
Then I tried walking in a Groucho Marx slouch.

"Stand up straight!" said Grandma.

"Can't!" I said, giggling. "My garter belt's too tight!"

"Well, glory," Grandma said, laughing. "Loosen it then!"

Dad was trying to look disapproving, but he couldn't help
smiling.

"You'd better get serious," he said, "if you're going to dance
in those things tonight without falling over."

I realized he was right. It would be horrible if I stumbled all
over and stepped on Mr. Davenport's toes while we were dancing. I thought again about staying home.

Grandma sensed my nervousness. "May I have this dance?"
she said, and she grabbed me and whirled me around the
kitchen in a waltz step, and I lurched along with her and we
both laughed. Dad was watching, and I could tell they were
both enjoying the sight of me in my first high heels, even if I
was in rag curlers and my old chenille bathrobe.

Grandma and I both sat down breathlessly in kitchen chairs.

"Your dad used to be a fine dancer," she said.

Dad looked embarrassed. I wondered if she was hinting something about Irene and the dance.

"He used to go out dancing with your momma all the time,"
she said. "Go on, James, you help Addie practice in her shoes."

She pushed me forward, and Dad looked a bit sheepish.
Then Grandma started humming a song, and he held out his
hand to me, and I took it, and we danced around the kitchen.

My dad was tall—as tall as Mr. Davenport. But with my
high heels on, I didn't have to stretch much to dance with

him. We both laughed when I stumbled a bit, but I was deter-
mined to get the hang of the darn shoes. Dad seemed to be
enjoying himself.

"Whew!" he said when we stopped. "I guess I haven't got
what it takes any more."

Grandma smiled.

"You look as good as you ever did on the dance floor," she
said.

Now I was sure she was hinting.

Dad ignored the remark. I tried to think of some way to
pursue the subject of Irene.

"Sit down here," said Grandma, "and I'll take your curlers
out."

She untied all the rag curlers, letting my hair fall down in
ringlets around my face.

"Looks like Irene did a real nice job on your permanent,"
Grandma said. "Curls up real good."

I saw Dad glance at her.

"Yeah," I said, sounding unimpressed. "I guess it's OK." I
wasn't going to give him the satisfaction of being enthusiastic
about Irene. He had to know that she was all wrong for him.

"What did you think of Irene?" asked Grandma, not realizing
she was playing right into my hands.

"I think she's very common," I said coolly, trying to catch a
glance of Dad's face without his seeing me. I saw him move
uncomfortably in the doorway.

"That's not a very nice thing to say, Addie," said Grandma.

"Well, she is!" I said hotly. My feet were jiggling up and
down nervously. "She wears that la-de-da hair-do, and I bet it's
bleached blond too, and those wedgies, and all that red nail
polish! I think she's absolutely trashy!" I wanted him to know
just how I felt.

"Addie!" said Grandma. "I don't want to hear you talk like that about anybody!"

"I'm going to be late!" I said, and jumped up from the chair, pulling out the last of the curlers and dumping them on the table. I headed for the bedroom. As I left the room, I heard Grandma speaking to Dad.

"You're not going to the dance?" she asked him.

"You heard that," he said. "Addie would have a fit."

I stood in front of the mirror and gave myself a triumphant look. Irene had invited him to the dance, and I had successfully kept him from going. I was very pleased with myself. The whole idea of the two of them seeing each other was absolutely ridiculous.

I pulled on my dress and clasped Grandma's rhinestone bracelet around my wrist. Then I slowly brushed out my hair. I hated to admit it, but Irene had done a good job on it. She had styled it into a long page boy, slightly fluffed out at the ends, and I did look older and more attractive.

"Come out and let's see," Grandma called from the kitchen.

I took one last look at myself in the mirror. Would it be enough for Mr. Davenport?

I walked slowly out to the kitchen and stood in the doorway. Neither Dad nor Grandma said a thing. They just looked at me as though they had never seen me before. I felt like a freak.

"I'm not going to the stupid dance!" I shouted, and wheeled around and ran back into the bedroom.

I threw myself on the bed. I wasn't going to the dance and let everybody laugh at me for trying to look glamorous. It just wasn't me, and I wasn't going to be the only one there without a date.

Dad and Grandma came into the bedroom.

"Why, Addie!" Grandma said. "Of course you're going to

the dance. You look so pretty—you can't stay home and let all this go to waste."

"I'm not going," I said.

"I already paid for your ticket," said Dad.

"Now, James," said Grandma.

"Well, she's got a new dress and shoes and a permanent—Lord knows what all that costs," he said.

"Money ain't the thing that's important here," said Grandma firmly.

"Well, you know what I mean," said Dad.

"You look fine, Addie," said Grandma. "There's no reason why you shouldn't go."

"I'm not going," I repeated. "I'm not going to be the only one there without a date."

"Well, I'll take you myself," Dad said suddenly.

Grandma gave him a look.

"What?" I said.

"I'll go put on a suit," he said.

"You don't have to dress up just to walk her over there," Grandma said slyly, watching him.

"Well, I might stay a few minutes," he mumbled, and turned and left the room.

"I can't go with you!" I called after him, but he'd already headed for his room. "I can't go with my own father! My gosh, that would be awful," I mumbled to Grandma.

"Addie," said Grandma. "It's nice he wants to take you. You mustn't hurt his feelings."

I sat there quietly for a moment, wondering if Dad really wanted to take me to the dance or if he had changed his mind about seeing Irene. He must be putting on the suit for her. The whole evening was going to be a total disaster. Me with no date, looking like a silly thirteen-year-old trying to be grown-up in front of Mr. Davenport; Billy with Tanya; and my father with Irene Davis in front of everyone! I wanted to hide under the bed.

Just then Dad came back into the room with a little white box. He handed it to me.

"Here," he said. "I thought you ought to wear this with your fancy dress."

I opened it, and inside was a corsage of white daisies. It was the first time my father had ever bought me anything like that. I couldn't think of what to say. I was almost sorry I had been so nasty about Irene.

I took the flowers out and Grandma pinned them on my dress.

"Thanks, Dad," I said.

"OK," he said, looking embarrassed, and he went to his room to put on his good blue suit.

I looked at myself in the mirror and admired the flowers. I decided I didn't look half bad. Maybe I could carry it off after all.

Chapter Seven.

I WAS REALLY EMBARRASSED to walk into the gym with my father. It was worse than going to the dance with no date, and I wanted to run ahead so no one would see I was with him, but I didn't want to hurt his feelings.

Luckily the gym was rather dark. So much crepe paper hung from the rafters that it cut out most of the big ceiling lights.

As we walked in the door, several of the kids looked over at us, but nobody said anything. I saw Mr. Davenport in a group of adults at the other end of the gym. I breathed a sigh of relief when I saw his back was turned. It would have been humiliating to have him see my father bringing me to the dance as though I were a child.

I saw Billy, Tanya, Carla Mae, and some of the other kids across the floor by the record player, and I said good-bye to Dad and started over to join them. Suddenly I saw Irene coming toward me.

"Hello, Addie," she said, smiling. "Your hair looks real nice."

"Thanks," I said, wanting to avoid her.

"Pretty flowers," she said, looking at my corsage. "Daisies are my favorite."

I looked at her and wondered just for a second if Dad had bought the corsage for her before he changed his mind about going to the dance.

Then Irene saw Dad behind me and stopped smiling. She gave him a very annoyed look, and as I turned to see what was happening, I saw him looking at her with a pained expression. She brushed past me and stood close to him, but I could hear every word they said to each other.

"I thought you didn't want to come to the dance!" she said angrily.

"I had to walk Addie over," he said, looking sheepish.

"Well, how come you wouldn't come with me when I asked you then? Are you ashamed to be seen with me?"

"Oh, don't be silly, Irene," he said.

"Well, you've never asked me to go out any place in this town—just in places where you'll be sure nobody will see us."

I couldn't believe it. Actually seeing them together horrified me. I had always daydreamed that Dad might get married again, but to someone elegant and sophisticated—not someone as common as Irene.

Dad saw me watching them and looked troubled. I walked away, leaving the two of them standing there. It was embarrassing enough that I was there with no date, but now everybody would see my father with Irene. I wanted to drop through the floor.

I started toward the record player again, and Tanya pulled Billy out onto the dance floor as though she were trying to avoid me. Carla Mae and her date, Jimmy Walsh, were selecting records for the next few dances.

"Addie!" she said. "You look great. Love your heels!"

"Thanks," I said. "Yours are neat, too."

"Your hair really looks different," said Jimmy.

"Yeah, it's OK, I guess," I said. I wasn't paying much attention to the two of them; I was straining to see who Mr. Davenport was talking to and watching Tanya and Billy out of the corner of my eye. Tanya, always the great ballerina, kept swishing her dress around and doing a lot of fancy steps, looking to see if everyone was watching her. Billy looked uncomfortable.

Carla Mae saw me watching them.

"Listen, Addie," she said. "I have to tell you something."

"What?"

She drew me aside so no one else could hear.

"You should hear what Billy said about you when you came in."

"What?" I asked, feeling angry. He had probably said something insulting.

"You mean you really want to know?" Carla Mae asked, teasing me.

"Carter, if you don't tell me, I'll strangle you!"

"OK. He said you looked really neat!"

"He did?" I found that puzzling. I didn't know what to make of it. I thought he was angry at me.

"Is that all?" I asked. "Did he say anything else?"

"Well, he said you were one of the best-looking ones here."

"He did? In front of Tanya?"

"No," said Carla Mae. "Just so I could hear it. Listen, he knew I'd tell you. He knows we always tell each other everything."

"He's so sneaky sometimes!" I said, pleased. If Billy thought I looked good, I was more encouraged about approaching Mr. Davenport. I decided that now was the time to go and say hello to him.

Just then Jimmy put a conga record on and everyone rushed to form lines. I saw Irene pulling my father's hand and dragging him out on the dance floor. I had never seen him at a dance before, and he actually looked as if he was enjoying himself.

Irene started one line with him and moved it around the floor quickly, laughing and shouting to the others as she went by. The other lines joined hers one by one until there were thirty or forty people dancing in one long line around the gym. I couldn't believe my father was making such a fool of himself. I had always wanted him to be less stern and quiet than he was, but now that I saw him that way I hated it. I squashed myself as far back into the corner by the record player as I could and hoped no one could see me.

Mr. Davenport was watching the conga line, too, and I hoped he didn't recognize my father with Irene. When the conga was over, I once again made ready to approach him, but he started to move toward the stage and the microphone that had been set up there. It was time for the crowning of the King and Queen of Hearts. It all seemed so silly and unimportant to me; I was anxious for them to get it over with so I could talk to Mr. Davenport.

The stage was decorated with crepe paper streamers, too, and in the center were two huge throne chairs we had borrowed from the local Baptist church. Draped across each chair was an "ermine" robe of cotton we had all made in art class, and on each robe rested the foil-covered crowns we had designed. Big red cardboard hearts, covered with glitter, hung all over the stage as a backdrop.

Carla Mae and Jimmy had come back to the corner by the record player, and we stood watching together.

"I don't know what the big suspense is," Carla Mae said. "Everybody knows it's Billy Wild and Carolyn Holt."

"Well," said Jimmy. "She is the prettiest one in the class."

"I know," I said. "That's the point. Everybody knows she's the prettiest, so we all vote for her for stuff like this and she wins every time and there's never any suspense."

"Yeah," said Jimmy. "You're right. Billy always wins, too, because he's the best in sports."

"Also he's the cutest," said Carla Mae.

"Oh, really!" I said. "It's all so adolescent."

"Well, we are adolescent!" said Carla Mae irritably.

"Speak for yourself," I said.

At a signal from Mr. Davenport, Irene sat down at the piano on stage and played a little fanfare.

"Ladies and gentlemen!" said Mr. Davenport. "Now for the highlight of the evening, we are proud to announce the King and Queen of Hearts for 1949. The result of secret balloting by the entire seventh-grade class."

Everyone in the class applauded themselves as he said that.

Mr. Davenport took an envelope out of his pocket and removed a sheet of paper with the results on it.

He made a dramatic pause, then announced, "The King and Queen of Hearts are—Billy Wild and Carolyn Holt!"

Carla Mae and I gave each other mock looks of surprise and then applauded and cheered loudly. We liked Carolyn and had voted for her ourselves, so we were pleased. I had even voted for Billy, in spite of the fact that he was obnoxious.

Billy and Carolyn made their way up the steps to the stage, Carolyn looking modestly pleased and Billy looking embarrassed. Mr. Davenport draped the ermine robes around each of them and carefully placed the crowns on their heads. Then Irene played "Heart of My Heart," without jazzing it up too much. And Carolyn's mother came up to the foot of the stage and took a flash picture.

I was watching Mr. Davenport.

"Oh, this is going to go on forever," I said to Carla Mae. "I wish we would get on with the dance."

Tanya moved in beside us.

"I just knew he'd win," she gushed. "I'm so proud of him."

"Proud of him?" said Carla Mae. "What did you have to do with it?"

"Well, I *am* his date!" said Tanya.

"Oh, brother!" said Carla Mae, and she and I rolled our eyes at each other.

"Now," Mr. Davenport said. "The King and Queen will have the first part of this dance. Then when the music stops they'll choose other partners, and each time the music stops, those who are dancing please choose new partners."

"Oh, good," said Tanya. "I get to dance with Billy with his crown on. I hope my mother gets a picture."

Carla Mae and I smirked at each other.

Someone put "My Funny Valentine" on the record player, and Billy and Carolyn, both looking awkward in their robes and crowns, started dancing alone in the middle of the floor. Somebody turned on a spotlight from the stage and followed them around the floor with it.

In a few moments the music stopped, and Billy and Carolyn started to move toward the edge of the floor to choose new partners. Carolyn asked Dick Peterson, who was her date, and Billy headed toward our corner. Tanya started adjusting her dress, ready to get out on the floor and show off again.

"Addie," she said. "Are my seams straight?"

I checked the back of her legs. "One of them looks like a corkscrew," I lied.

"Oh, no!" she said. "It would happen now." She craned her neck around to see what was wrong with her stocking, and Carla Mae and I broke up laughing.

Just then Billy walked up to us.

"Hi, Addie," he said. "Wanna dance?"

Tanya turned back toward us so fast I thought her neck would snap.

I was about to say no to Billy when I saw the look on Tanya's face. She couldn't believe it.

"Sure," I said to Billy, and we moved out to the dance floor.

We stalked around stiffly for a few moments, with Carolyn and Dick dancing just as self-consciously across the floor from us. The spotlight in our eyes made it difficult to see where we were going, and I was thankful there was only one other couple to worry about bumping into on the floor. Billy's robe kept getting in the way, and his crown would slip over his forehead each time we changed directions.

"I think you were supposed to ask Tanya to dance," I said.

"Are you kidding?" Billy said. "She's been dancing with everybody else in the place. All she does is show off what a hot dancer she is. It's like trying to drag a tornado around the floor."

"Serves him right," I thought, but I didn't say it.

I twisted around a bit to see if I could spot Mr. Davenport. I wished the music would stop so I could go and choose him as my next partner.

"You look neat," Billy was saying.

I didn't reply.

"I was really going to ask you to the dance," he said. "But you made me so mad that day after class—well, I just asked Tanya to get even."

"It doesn't matter," I said. "I didn't even want to come to the dumb dance anyway."

"Well, I wish I hadn't either," he said. "I really feel stupid in this get-up."

"Yes," I said, looking at him. "It's pretty childish."

Before he could reply the music stopped, and I quickly dropped his hand.

"Thanks," he said, starting to walk me off the floor.

"Sure," I said as I left him standing there and started toward Mr. Davenport.

Now I was going to find out what it was he wanted to tell me. That, after all, was my only reason for coming to the dance.

He smiled as I walked up to him.

"Hello, Addie," he said. "You look wonderful."

"So do you," I blurted out. He was wearing a handsome blue suit and a wonderful tie with navy and red stripes. I was staring at it and wondering if I could remember just the color of blue to try in a painting of him when I realized he was introducing me to someone standing next to him. I looked up.

". . . Kathleen Tate," he was saying. "My fiancée."

I heard the word, but it didn't register at first. I could see it in front of me. I knew it was a French word with two e's at the end, an accent over the next to last one. I always won the spelling bee in our class.

I was reaching out my hand to shake hands with her and saying, "Hello, nice to meet you," but it seemed to be coming from somewhere else.

"Kathleen and I are going to be married this June when school's out," he said. "But don't tell anyone yet; it's still our secret. She's teaching in Omaha. I wanted you two to meet. I knew you'd like each other."

Kathleen gave me a dazzling smile. She was beautiful.

"I'm delighted to meet you, Addie," she said. "Douglas has told me so much about you and your interest in art. I think you're his favorite student!"

"Thank you," I mumbled.

"I hope you were coming over to ask me to dance, Addie," said Mr. Davenport, smiling.

"Oh, yeah," I said.

He took my hand and we moved to the dance floor. I looked back at Kathleen. I knew I must be invisible next to someone as beautiful as she was, and I felt like a fool for trying so hard to look glamorous.

"I've taken a job teaching in Kansas City for next year," he was saying. "We finally found a place where we can both teach in the same school."

"Oh, great," I said numbly.

When the music stopped, Mr. Davenport thanked me and started to walk me to the side of the dance floor, but I left him standing there and headed back for the corner by the record player where Carla Mae and some of the other girls were standing.

Someone put on another record, and everyone moved to the floor to dance.

"You were dancing with Alan Ladd!" Carla Mae giggled.

I was silent.

"Did you see his girlfriend?" she said.

"Yeah."

"Is she gorgeous? Oh, I'd give my arm to look like that."

"Well if you gave your arm, you wouldn't look like that, would you?" I asked irritably.

"What's the matter with you?" she asked.

"Nothing!" I said angrily.

Jimmy asked Carla Mae to dance, and they went out on the floor. I stood there by myself watching them. Billy and Tanya were dancing together again and so were Carolyn and Dick and my father and Irene. Mr. Davenport was dancing very close with Kathleen.

I realized I was the only person there who wasn't with some-one. I was the only one alone. I suddenly felt everyone was watching me. I felt paralyzed. If I only had gloves or a handker-chief to fiddle with, something to look busy with. I bent over to fix the seam of one of my stockings and I heard someone whistle. Three of the boys in our class were sitting on the edge of the bleacher seats, watching me. They whistled again, rudely.

"Oh, shut up!" I said to them.

"Hey, glamor girl," one of them called to me. "You got a great pair of legs!"

None of the boys in our class had ever said anything like that to me before, and I was furious. They were mocking me some-how, trying to embarrass me for having tried to look good. I hated them for it.

"Just shut up!" I repeated.

"Whatcha gonna do, kick me with your high heels?" one of them said sarcastically,

"You're disgusting!" I said. At that, they all roared with laughter.

"Disgusting!" one of them shrieked, mocking me.

I was so angry that without thinking I grabbed a basketball that was sitting on the bleachers and heaved it at one of them. He just laughed and caught it, and tossed it to one of the others.

Suddenly one of them started bouncing it on the gym floor toward the basket and took a shot. He missed.

"Bad shot!" I said, pleased that he had failed at showing off.

"Let's see you do better," he said and threw the ball at me angrily.

I caught it easily. I was a whiz at basketball, and I wasn't about to let them humiliate me for another second. I kicked off my shoes, put my corsage on the bleachers, then dribbled a couple of steps, and made a perfect one-handed jump shot.

One of the other boys grabbed the ball under the basket and in a second I was in the middle of an impromptu basketball game with them, all thoughts of high heels and taunting remarks left behind.

A couple of the other boys standing along the sidelines joined in, and without realizing it we had broken up the whole dance. I was lurching around wildly under the basket, sliding in my nylon stockings, my dress flying. We weren't even aware that Mr. Davenport was striding across the floor toward us.

"All right," he shouted. "That's enough!"

We kept right on playing.

"That's enough!" he said angrily. "Stop this now!"

We stopped, and the boys withdrew to the sides of the gym. I was left standing under the basket, holding the ball.

"This is a dance, not a basketball game!" Mr. Davenport said, looking at me.

Everybody was staring at me, and my face was burning.

I turned away and went to put my shoes back on.

"Addie, I'm surprised at you," he said, following me. "What a childish thing to do."

Nothing he could have said would have hurt me more than that.

"Well, I'd rather play basketball than dance any day!" I said, close to tears. I knew I had made a fool of myself in front of him, and I ran for the door.

"Addie . . ." Mr. Davenport called after me, but I rushed past him and out the door.

Chapter Eight

I TOOK THE SHORTCUT through the playground, heading for our house, which was only two blocks away. I heard someone call my name, and I looked around. Dad was coming toward me from the schoolhouse door, carrying my coat.

I sat down in one of the swings and waited for him, tears running down my face.

"Is that any way to behave at a dance?" he asked as he approached me.

"I don't care. I'm going home."

"Why'd you run out like that?"

"That stupid Mr. Davenport. He embarrassed me in front of everybody! Calling me childish!"

"Well, what in the world are you doing playing basketball at a dance?"

"They started it!" I said, still crying.

He put the coat over my shoulders and sat down in the swing next to me.

"Being called down is nothing to get so upset over," he said, handing me his handkerchief.

"I hate this dance!" I said, blowing my nose noisily. "I hate looking like this! It's not me!"

"I think you look real nice," he said.

"It's disgusting!" I said angrily. "Those boys are so stupid and mean! They whistled at me like a bunch of idiots. It made me feel awful."

"They don't mean any harm," he said. "Sometimes boys act foolish. They don't know what to say to girls. It's just as hard for them."

"Well, they're all creeps!"

"I thought you were having a good time. I saw you dancing with Billy Wild and Mr. Davenport . . ."

"I can't stand Mr. Davenport!"

"I thought you liked him a lot."

"No!"

"Irene said his girlfriend was there. Did you meet her?"

"It's not his girlfriend," I said. "It's his fiancée."

"Oh, he's getting married," said Dad.

"Yeah, this June. And moving away to Kansas City."

"I guess you'll miss him. All the kids seem to like him."

"I don't care what he does," I said and got up from the swing and started to walk toward home.

Dad walked along beside me.

"It's unfair," I said after a few moments. "The pretty girls get everything without even trying. If you're not beautiful or rich, then you're nobody. It's just not fair—they get everything! Everybody falls in love with them!"

"Well, love isn't something you 'get,'" said Dad. "It's not like winning a game or something. It doesn't happen at first sight. You have to know somebody a long time and work at it."

"Yeah, but if boys don't like the way you look, you never get

the chance to know them. That's all they care about. And you're
the same way with that Irene Davis!"

"Irene's a nice person," he said. "I wanted to tell you I was
going out with her, but I just didn't know what to say . . ."

"How could you like somebody like that?" I asked. "She's
so—I don't know—she's not refined like my mother was."

"No," said Dad. "She's not much like your mother, but that
doesn't mean we can't like each other."

I wondered how he could say that. I imagined that his love
for my mother had been like the feeling I had for Mr. Davenport. We walked along for a moment, not saying anything.

"I don't suppose I'll ever feel that way about anybody again,"
he said. "The way I felt about your mother . . ."

I was surprised that he continued the conversation. He almost never mentioned my mother to me. What little I knew
of her I had learned from Grandma.

"But that doesn't mean I can't enjoy other people's company," he went on. "And care about them in a different way."

"But it's not the same," I said.

"No," he said. "It's not, but you don't always get just what
you want in life."

"I don't see why not," I said impatiently. That had always
been an argument between us. I thought you could make things
happen the way you wanted in life, and he was a firm believer
in fate, not to mention bad luck.

"You just can't settle for any old thing that comes along," I
said. "Then you'll never get what you really want. You have to
try for it."

It struck me that I was repeating what Mr. Davenport had
said to me about trying to be an artist. It was true that my dad
was disappointed about some things in his life, and it was a

constant struggle for me to overcome his pessimism and maintain my optimism. As badly as I felt about Mr. Davenport, I somehow knew that I didn't share Dad's pessimism about love.

He didn't say anything for a moment, as though he were thinking over what I had said.

"I don't know," he said thoughtfully. "Sometimes I thought if I couldn't find somebody like your mother again I'd rather be alone. But I'm pretty sure there's nobody else like her for me, and I don't think I want to be alone the rest of my life—that doesn't seem right either."

I had never thought of it that way, and it made me very sad to think of anyone, especially my dad, settling for something he didn't really want just to keep from being alone.

"I don't have all the answers," he said. "I guess you just have to try and see what happens. You can't just give up the first time something goes wrong."

He looked over at me, and I knew he was referring to Mr. Davenport.

"There're plenty of boys around for you to like, that's for sure," he said.

"I don't know who," I said dejectedly. "I don't know how you're ever supposed to *find* anybody."

"Well, you don't exactly go out and *look* for somebody," he said. "You just have to keep your eyes open to what's happening around you. The right person might be there all along and you wouldn't see him—somebody like Billy."

"Oh, him. He didn't even ask me to the dance," I said.

"That doesn't mean he doesn't like you," said Dad.

"I guess not," I said, and wondered how Billy really did feel. I had hardly talked to him at the dance, and he had been very nice to me after all. I wondered if I had hurt his feelings, and I realized it was the first time that night I had even thought about his feelings, I had been so preoccupied with my own.

"I asked Irene to come over to the house for coffee," Dad said.

I looked up, surprised.

"I think you ought to try to get to know her," he said. "I think you'll like her. She's a lot of fun . . ." His voice trailed off for a moment.

"It isn't always perfect, you know," he said. "It doesn't happen the way it says in the movies."

I looked closely at my father as we walked along together. I wondered if it was fair of me to wish he wouldn't settle for just anyone. I knew I could never do that. If I had been Grandma, I would have married Tom. I would do what I thought was right for me.

Chapter Nine

GRANDMA WAS SURPRISED to see us back from the dance so soon, but I didn't feel like explaining it all. I went into the bedroom to hang up my coat, and I heard Dad talking to her in the kitchen.

I put my coat in the closet Grandma and I shared, and stood there looking at myself in the mirror. I wondered if I would grow up to look anything like Kathleen, but I figured I had no chance. Grandma came in and stood next to me and put her arm around me.

"You didn't like the dance?"

"It wasn't any fun," I said.

"Your dad told me about the basketball game," she said.

"Oh."

"That must have been a sight," she said, smiling a bit.

"Yeah," I said. "I guess I acted really dumb."

"Oh, I don't know," she said.

"I wish I hadn't even gone," I said.

"Dad says Mr. Davenport's getting married," Grandma said.

"Yeah."

"Well, I guess your whole class will miss him."

"Yeah, I guess so," I said listlessly. "We'd have a different teacher next year anyway, so we'd probably never see him even if he was here."

I kicked off my high heels.

"Don't forget to put tissue in those to hold the shape," Grandma said. "You can wear them to the next big dance."

"Ugh," I said. "I'd rather wear army boots—these are so uncomfortable."

"Well, put them back on a minute and come out and have some cake and ice cream. Irene is here."

"Oh, no," I groaned. I had forgotten Irene was coming over. The last thing I wanted to do was sit around the kitchen table and be sociable with company—especially Irene Davis.

"Now, Addie," said Grandma. "You behave yourself. Come on."

We went into the kitchen, where Dad and Irene were sitting at the table having coffee and some of Grandma's chocolate cake. I poured myself a big glass of milk, and Grandma and I sat down, too. I was curious to see how Dad behaved around Irene, and I tried to watch them but didn't want to be rude or stare or anything. We were all a little uncomfortable, but Irene just kept chatting and laughing as if nothing was wrong.

"Just love your shoes and dress, Addie," she said.

"I hope I never have to wear them again," I said grumpily.

"Oh, you look great in them," she said. "Even playing basketball." She laughed.

For a second I was angry, then Dad and Grandma smiled, too, and I realized how funny I must have looked skidding around the gym in my dress and stocking feet, and I started to laugh too.

"You sure livened up the joint!" Irene said. "It was a pretty dull dance till you arrived!"

"Yeah," I said, and we all laughed again.

Somebody knocked on the kitchen door, and Grandma got up to answer it. I thought I heard Billy Wild's voice coming from the dark porch, and I went to the door too. He was standing there with a red satin, heart-shaped candy box tucked awkwardly under his arm.

"Hi," he said to me.

"Hi," I said. "How come you left the dance?"

"I didn't like it either," he said. "Tanya was dancing up a storm with everybody else, and she said she didn't care if I stayed or not, so I just left. Anyway," he said, talking very fast. "I had this over at my house and I just wanted to give it to you since tomorrow is Valentine's Day and I didn't send out cards or anything."

He quickly shoved the box at me, and I took it.

"Thanks," I said. No one had ever given me a box of candy before in my life.

"Well, Billy, come in and have a piece of cake with us," Grandma said.

"Yeah," I said. "You might as well, now that you're here."

Billy joined us at the table, and I cut a big piece of cake for him and poured him a glass of milk.

"Well, it's not very often I get to sit down to the table with a king," laughed Irene. "Congratulations, Billy."

"Thanks," he said, and blushed.

"You're not a bad dancer, either," Irene said to him. "I saw you flittin' around out there."

I had a feeling Irene was building him up to impress me, but I wasn't quite sure. Billy seemed embarrassed, but Irene took no notice and rattled on.

"I remember my high school prom," she said. "I invited a boy I just barely knew from another town, and when we went

out on the dance floor, it turned out his town did the two-step different than our town." She laughed. "Well, you shoulda seen us staggering around that floor—like two hogs on ice. Couldn't get together to save our souls!"

She had a big, contagious laugh, and we were all laughing with her by the time she finished. I could see what Dad had meant about her being a lot of fun.

And I could see a change in him. He looked more relaxed and happy than I could remember in a long time. I thought of the snapshots in our family photo album; pictures of him and my mother before I was born—they were fishing, hiking, sleigh-riding—happy and enjoying themselves. I had seldom seen that carefree side of Dad, but I thought I saw a touch of it now. I felt a moment of jealousy that Irene had been able to do that for him and I hadn't. But then I knew I could laugh with someone like Billy about things Dad would never understand. It really wasn't something to be jealous about, and I was glad Irene was there.

Billy seemed to have caught the storytelling bug from Irene.

"You should have seen us trying to dance in the spotlight," Billy said to Grandma. "They had this dumb light right in our eyes so we couldn't see where we were going, and I kept trip-ping over my robe and my crown kept slipping."

He got up and demonstrated for Grandma, stumbling around the kitchen floor. He was so funny that she laughed and laughed, and the rest of us did too, until I thought we would choke on our chocolate cake.

"Then Addie made a terrific basket," he said. "A one-handed jump shot."

"Did you see that?" I asked, rather proud he had noticed it.

"Yeah, it was neat."

"Mr. Davenport didn't think so," I said quietly.

"Listen," said Irene. "That Mr. Davenport is a little on the stuffy side if you ask me. I thought the basketball game was the best part of the whole dance."

"Yeah," said Billy, laughing. "Me, too!"

I went over to the counter and got the box of candy he had brought and put it on the table. Everyone admired it, and I opened it and we all had some. Dad said our teeth would fall out from all the sweets, which was the kind of thing he always said, and Grandma said Valentine's Day was only once a year, which was the kind of thing she always said.

Then I went into the bedroom, unlocked my private drawer and took out the special valentine I had made for Mr. Davenport.

As I removed it, the scent of Mr. Davenport's Rum and Maple tobacco wafted up toward me, and I felt suddenly wounded. What a stupid thing to have kept someone's tobacco!

I grabbed the knotted handkerchief and ran to the window with it. I opened the window wide, untied the knot and thrust the handkerchief out into the cold. A gust of wind fluttered it, and the loose tobacco drifted away in the night air. I closed the window with a bang and pressed the handkerchief to my face. It still smelled like Rum and Maple, I thought, annoyed, but I knew it would wash out.

I went back to the dresser and picked up the valentine. I looked at Mr. Davenport's name on the envelope for a moment. I took out the valentine. I had worked on it for hours. It was layer upon layer of hearts, made in alternating pieces of red paper, lace doily, tin foil, red glitter, white glitter and red velvet, with white and red ribbons laced all through it. The bottom heart was the largest, with each one on top progressively smaller, so that it had a fantastic three-dimensional effect. On the top heart it said simply "Be My Valentine, From Addie."

I had not wanted an elaborate verse to detract from my design.

I put it down carefully on the dresser, then picked up the envelope with Mr. Davenport's name on it and tore it up into little pieces. I took another envelope from my valentine box and wrote "To The King of Hearts, From Addie" on it.

I went back to the kitchen. Billy was still at the table, joking and talking and trying to help Irene figure out which chocolate was a coconut cream.

I looked at him and thought about how we had been friends for so many years. There was even a snapshot in our family album of my first birthday party, and Billy was one of the guests, bawling his head off while I was busy plunging my fist into the cake. We had shared a double desk in kindergarten. We went to the same Sunday School class, rode horses together, quarrelled, giggled, and competed with each other for nearly thirteen years. Maybe Dad had a point. Billy had been there all along, and I was so used to seeing him that I hadn't really taken a good look at him.

I motioned to him to join me over by the door, and he left the table. I shoved the envelope at him the same way he had given me the box of candy.

"Don't open this till you get home," I said.

"Thanks," he said, and gave me a big grin.

Then Billy and I went back to the table, and we all clinked our coffee cups and glasses of milk together and wished each other a Happy Valentine's Day.

Epilogue

BILLY AND I were good friends all through high school. I learned not to take his friendship for granted, and he treated me with the same regard. When we went away to different universities, we wrote letters and saw each other in the summer. Then I went off to New York to become an artist and Billy married a girl he met in college. But we still keep in touch. We're still friends, and I think we always will be.

I never saw Mr. Davenport again after he moved away. In a few years I had to look at the class picture to remember his face, but I would never forget how I had felt about him.

I knew Dad had been right. Feeling something for other people was the important thing, even if it didn't always work out the way you thought it would.

When I realized that, I knew I was beginning to grow up— that Valentine's Day in 1949.

ABOUT THE AUTHOR

Gail Rock grew up in Valley, Nebraska, a small town not unlike the Clear River of this book. After receiving at B.A. in fine arts from the University of Nebraska, she moved to New York and began a career in journalism. She has worked at *Women's Wear Daily* as a film and TV critic and has done freelance writing for newspapers and magazines, including *Ms.* magazine. Gail Rock currently writes TV scripts and is working on a motion picture screenplay.

Addie and the King of Hearts, shown for the first time as a CBS Television Special simultaneously with the book's publication, is the fourth book about Addie Mills. The other books, *The House Without a Christmas Tree, The Thanksgiving Treasure,* and *A Dream for Addie* (televised as "The Easter Promise") have been warmly received. These stories were also television Specials, and they continue to be shown yearly. "The House Without a Christmas Tree" received a Christopher Award for its presentation.